Mary Blount Christian

SEBASTIAN (Super Sleuth) and the Clumsy Cowboy

Illustrated by LISA McCUE

MACMILLAN PUBLISHING COMPANY

New York

COLLIER MACMILLAN PUBLISHERS

London

For the Hicks family at the Mayan Dude Ranch,
who furnished the scenery without the
pandemonium!

Copyright © 1985 Mary Blount Christian
Copyright © 1985 Macmillan Publishing Company,
a division of Macmillan, Inc.
Macmillan Publishing Company
866 Third Avenue, New York, N.Y. 10022
Collier Macmillan Canada, Inc.
Printed in the United States of America
10 9 8 7 6 5 4 3 2 1
Library of Congress Cataloging in Publication Data
Christian, Mary Blount.
Sebastian (super sleuth) and the clumsy cowboy.
(Sebastian, super sleuth)
Summary: Dog detective Sebastian goes on an enforced
vacation to a seemingly haunted dude ranch.
1. Children's stories, American. [1. Mystery and
detective stories. 2. Dogs—Fiction] I. McCue,
Lisa, ill. II. Title. III. Series: Christian, Mary
Blount. Sebastian (super sleuth).
PZ7.C4528Set 1985 [Fic] 84-21758
ISBN 0-02-718480-3

7075371

Contents

1
In Trouble Again

Sebastian crawled under Chief's desk, his lip curled in a soft whimper. He'd never seen Chief so angry before. And all of that anger was directed at him and John!

Wham! Chief's fist hit the desk, just above the hairy hawkshaw's head. "That stupid mutt! That —that four-legged disaster! How *could* you, Detective John Quincy Jones?"

"B-b-but—" John sounded like an out-of-gas motorboat.

"How *could* you take that miserable fleabag to the stables of those Thoroughbred racehorses? Didn't you *know* he'd make a mess of things?"

Sebastian raised his head indignantly. Mess? Who'd found the ransom note after every cop on the force had searched for days? Just the greatest detective on four legs, that's who! And who gave him the proper credit? Nobody, that's who!

Imagine, they thought he'd had the ransom note in his mouth because it smelled like barbecue! They thought it had been an accident. (Well, even accidents count, don't they?) The note, made of letters cut from an unfamiliar newspaper—which indicated that the horse was being kept out of town —demanded a million dollars for the safe return of the horse, Royal Pain-in-the-Neck. It was one of the two clues they had in the horsenapping.

The second clue—and an important one, Sebastian felt—was the absence of Royal's goat. Racehorses are highstrung, so owners often let a goat, or maybe a dog (should some unemployed dog go for such a boring and thankless job!), live with the horses to keep them calm. Since Royal's goat, Snuffy, was missing, too, it was probably someone in the racing field who had taken the horse.

Chief's voice rose three decibels. "Didn't you know that it was like putting a Tasmanian devil in a room full of crystal?" *Wham!* His fist hit the desk again.

"B-b-but, Chief!" John stammered. "I—I—"

Sebastian tried to make himself disappear into a ball of fur. Way to go, John. That was really telling him! That was speaking up for his loyal, trustworthy, and fantastic furry detective partner!

Hadn't he, Sebastian (Super Sleuth), with his

cunning ability to sift through clues, solved the baffling cases time after time for his human? John was the official police detective, that is, the only one in the family actually paid for his work. But it was the clever canine who solved the mysteries.

Chief's heavy shoes stomped near Sebastian's sensitive nose, as he paced back and forth in an outburst of rage. "That bungling bundle of hair actually nipped the heel of a Thoroughbred race-horse. I don't know why you can't control that dog any better!"

"B-b-b—" John stuttered.

Sebastian curled his lip in a snarl. Could he help it if someone had put another horse, Numb's the Word, into the stall of the kidnapped horse? And could he help it if the dumb animal had stepped between him and half of a bologna sand-wich on the floor of the stall? Even a dumb horse should know you don't come between a ravenous detective and his nourishment!

Sebastian sniffed. Speaking of nourishment, was that a chicken salad sandwich he smelled? He sniffed again. The delicious smell was coming from the top of Chief's filing cabinet. Cautiously, he crept over toward it, avoiding Chief's size 13 shiny black shoes.

"You were supposed to be investigating a horsenapping for ransom. Instead, you turned the stables into a shambles. Why, that horse kicked the door down when your fleabag bit him!"

Fleabag! *Errrrr.* Sebastian rumbled low in his throat. He rose on his hind legs until he was nose to sandwich. He snapped up the chicken salad sandwich and swallowed it whole. One must fight back as best one can!

"Get that—that walking garbage disposal out of here!" Chief yelled. "You're off this case! You have some personal time coming. Do us all a favor and take it! I don't want to see either of your faces until Monday."

"But, Chief!" John protested. "Didn't I find the ransom note—one of only two clues we have so far? And you said the entire force had to work around the clock until we got that million-dollar racehorse back. You even wanted us to find it before the race on Tuesday!"

Sebastian glared at John. Taking all the credit for finding that note was shameful! Someday the public would know the truth! He had a good mind to write his memoirs, expose everything. If only those typewriter keys weren't too small for his paws.

Chief sputtered. "Getting you two out of my hair for the whole weekend is like adding an entire detective squad. Now, out of my office! Out!"

Sebastian trotted out, head held proudly high. He kept John between himself and Chief, just in case Chief decided to throw something. He did have a temper!

John sighed. "I—I just can't understand Chief," he muttered. "Why, being told to take a couple of days off at a time like this is like being suspended."

Sebastian touched his cold nose to John's hand to comfort him. Maybe they (he) could solve the case, anyway. They (he) didn't have to be on the department's payroll to get the job done. He was the living, four-legged proof of that.

"Oh, Sebastian, old pal," John said as he opened the car door. "Maybe it's time I looked for different work, something nine-to-five. Something that would let me settle down, have a normal life."

Sebastian whimpered. No, John, no! He particularly didn't like the sound of the words *settle down*. They made a high-spirited bachelor canine such as himself nervous. And if John meant settle down as in marriage, well, Sebastian wasn't ready to share his human.

If only he could speak John's language! How could he make his friend understand that detective work was in their blood? Their city needed them, whether Chief realized it or not!

He had to get John back in Chief's good graces before John, in his state of depression, did something stupid—like ask Maude Culpepper to marry him. And he knew just how to do it. He, Sebastian (Super Sleuth), had a horse to locate and a kidnapper to bring to justice!

2
A Ghost of a Chance

Sebastian was ready for a two-inch T-bone consolation. After all, he'd never been so humiliated before, never been driven out of the police station in a state of disgrace. (At least, not recently!)

To his disgust, John stopped off not at T-Bone Heaven but at Maude Culpepper's. Her dog, Lady Sharon, greeted him by touching her cold nose to his. He made an extra effort to be polite—for John's sake—but got a whiff of her *Ode de Doggie* perfume and sneezed. *Ahhhoooey!* What an assault on a sensitive nose like his!

Lady Sharon brought her squeeze toy over and dropped it playfully at his feet. She wagged the stub of her tail, inviting him to a game of keep-away. With a rumbling mutter in his throat, he ignored her and trotted over to John.

Maude was draped around John's neck, com-

forting him. Sebastian wiggled in between them and put his head on John's lap. He glared at Maude out of the corner of his eye.

"I know how much you love your work, John," Maude said. "It's unfair of Chief to embarrass you this way because of something Sebastian did. Couldn't you just promise to leave him at home— at least until the case is solved?"

Sebastian curled his lip at her and wiggled some more, forcing her to move over. Busybody! And just how did she expect the case to be solved without his expert assistance?

"Actually, Sebastian was a great help in this case," John said. "If it hadn't been for my old pal here, I'd never have found the ransom note. It must have fallen off the wall—the tack was still there—and was in the hay on the stall floor."

Sebastian smirked. Attaboy, John! Give the old super sleuth his due!

"Of course, it did smell a bit like barbecue. That might have had something to do with his fascination with the note," John added, much to Sebastian's dismay.

John heaved a heavy sigh. "The kidnapper wants a million dollars. If we—er, make that the police—don't come up with the culprit, the owners will certainly pay the price. They feel the horse is worth much more than that."

Maude went into the kitchen. She returned with some coffee for herself and John and a couple of doggie tidbits for Sebastian and Lady Sharon. "Have you ever thought of being a *private* detective, John? I mean, it takes the same skills, doesn't it? And surely it isn't as dangerous."

Sebastian perked up his ears. Dangerous? Ha! Detectives laugh in the face of danger! Wait a minute—did she say private? A private eye? Your own boss, with no Chief to yell at you? What a dashing doggie private eye he'd make. He would help John just as he had on the police force, with his clever creation of illusion. (Hadn't he gone undercover as everything from a Gypsy girl to Santa Claus, including an airline attendant, a bearskin rug, and—most clever of disguises—an ordinary dog?) But they'd be free! No more grumpy Chief! Maybe Maude wasn't such a bad sort, after all. She did have a good idea there.

"Oh, I suppose it takes the same skills. But I don't know—I like being in the police department. I really like my job, despite Chief. I'm not sure I'd like to be a private detective."

Maude grinned. "How would you like to find out? This weekend?"

John raised his eyebrow questioningly. "Now what are you getting at, Maude? *You* don't need a detective, do you?"

She laughed. "No, not me. But my aunt and uncle do. You know, I mentioned them before. Ethel and Bart Culpepper. They own the Bucking Bronc Dude Ranch about fifty miles west of the city."

Sebastian swallowed the last of his tidbit. Lady Sharon nosed one of hers toward him. No doubt she was trying to cut back. She was a bit overweight, he had noticed. Eagerly, he devoured that one, too, before easing closer to hear just what Maude Culpepper was suggesting.

"You're saying your aunt and uncle need a private detective?" John asked.

Maude nodded. "I—I really wanted to ask your help, anyway, but I knew how busy you were with this missing racehorse."

John frowned. "Well, I guess now I have the time. What's the problem?"

Maude got up and paced back and forth. "First, things started disappearing—little things, like bales of hay, rope, stuff like that. Of course, Aunt Ethel and Uncle Bart can't afford to lose a whole lot, but they weren't too worried. But now—" She threw up her hands. "Oh, John, you're going to think we're silly."

John leaned forward. "Yes? Now?"

Sebastian leaned forward, too, his ears cocked.

Maude let her hands drop to her sides. "Now

some of the guests are saying that the ranch has a—a—a ghost."

Sebastian felt the hair on his spine stand on end. A ghost? Weren't ghosts just pretend?

John burst out laughing. "Ghosts! Oh, Maude, I know you're trying to cheer me up. But can't you think of a better story than that?"

She sank to the couch again. "I was afraid you might laugh. That's the reason I didn't want to tell you. But Aunt Ethel and Uncle Bart are worried. The guests have been canceling, and without full occupancy in season, my aunt and uncle could lose the ranch. The local sheriff just laughed at them, but I hoped *you* wouldn't!"

John placed his hand on Maude's shoulder. "You're serious! Your aunt and uncle really think their ranch is haunted by a hay-stealing ghost?"

Sebastian broke into a panting grin. His fur smoothed back down.

"The least you could do is go with me to the dude ranch and see for yourself."

"Well," John said soothingly, "why don't I take Sebastian there and do whatever one does at a dude ranch? After all, I have the whole weekend off."

Sebastian moaned. Why did John agree to go to a dude ranch with Maude right now? Didn't he want to find the racehorse so Chief would stop being mad at them? Didn't he want to show Chief how wrong he was? Their place was there, in the city, doing their job, not out on the Bucking Bronc Dude Ranch with sticky cacti, coyotes, and bobcats bigger than dogs!

"I'll take enough dog food for both Sebastian and Lady Sharon," Maude said, hugging John's neck. "Go home and pack. Just comfortable stuff— jeans, shirts, and boots."

Dog food? She needn't bother on his account, Sebastian thought. Maybe Lady Sharon liked that yucky stuff. But the old gourmet would take ranch cooking, thank you—beef barbecued over an open pit all day, baked beans, ranch grits just oozing with cheese. Yummy! Or, as they say on a ranch, yippeeee-ti-yi! It could turn out to be a pleasant vacation.

Let Chief embarrass himself by not solving the case. Let Chief have to explain to the reporters and the horse's owners that he failed because he'd banished the dynamic duo from the investigation! That'd show him!

3
Meanwhile, at the Ranch

The hour's drive in Maude's station wagon was pleasant enough. Sebastian had never been in that area of the country. It seemed that no sooner had they left the confines of the city, with all its glass and concrete, than they came upon rolling hills filled with cedars, mesquite, and plants he'd never seen before.

Eventually, they turned onto a side road that snaked its way over a narrow bridge and through the foothills and pasture land, where horses munched on grass. They drove through an open wooden gate and up to a ranch house of sand-colored stone.

A tall man with a wreath of white hair and a big grin loped out to meet them, his arms extended toward Maude.

Lady Sharon bounced out of the car and balanced on her hind legs, yelping her greeting to the man. Sebastian decided to play it cool. He ambled from the wagon and strolled around casually, sniffing the setting to familiarize himself with it.

He rounded a low-slung mesquite bush and came to a quick stop. He was face to face with the biggest, weirdest bird he'd ever seen.

Ha-up! The bird sounded like a small child calling for help. It was eerie.

The man shook hands with John. "Peacocks," he explained. "We have about fifty pairs here. They keep the tourist area clear of rattlesnakes."

Sebastian's fur prickled. Rattlesnakes? Nobody had mentioned rattlesnakes. He eyed the bird cautiously. If that funny-looking bird could chase away rattlesnakes, it would bear watching.

A round woman with blue hair bounded out of the ranch house and hugged Maude warmly. Uncle Bart grabbed the luggage from the station wagon; he set it on the ground and motioned to a ranch hand. "Specks, luggage!"

The ranch hand, dressed in scruffy boots, jeans, and a checked shirt, came up. His face was covered with freckles. Sebastian cleverly concluded that this had earned Specks his name.

"John, you're in cabin fifteen. Maude is in thirty-seven. Supper is at seven o'clock," Uncle Bart said.

"We'll ring the dinner bell, just as a reminder."

Sebastian sniffed the air. It smelled of barbecue. That was all the reminder he needed!

"I'm so glad you came to solve our mystery for us, John," Aunt Ethel said. "It's driving away all our business at the worst time possible!"

"Well," John said, blushing, "I said I would look into it. I can't promise that I'll solve it. But usually these ghost things are easily explained."

Uncle Bart scratched his chin thoughtfully. "Well, I sure hope you can explain this one. It's the strangest thing we ever saw."

"You saw this—this ghost, too?" John said.

Aunt Ethel rolled her eyes. "Oh, did we! It was —well, it was—well, you'll just have to see it for yourselves."

"And I'm sure you will," Uncle Bart said. "It's been here every night for a week. We have no reason to think it won't be here tonight, too."

Ha-up! One of the peacocks spread its wings and fluttered to the lower branch of a pin oak tree.

Ha-up! Another answered from the bushes.

Sebastian felt the fur on his nape stand up. These birds were strange enough, with their spooky cry. But all this talk about ghosts, as if they really existed, was downright scary.

Lady Sharon edged closer to him, whimpering.

This time he didn't snarl at her. Maybe there was safety in numbers.

John whistled for Sebastian to follow. "Come on, fellow. Let's get settled in our cabin before supper."

The two of them followed Specks to their cabin. It was made of pine logs and stood on a knoll, overlooking a broad expanse of grassland. Only the tops of a few mesquite trees, about a hundred feet away from the cabin, obscured any of the view.

"Great view!" John said, inhaling the quickly cooling air and stretching vigorously.

Specks shoved his Western hat to the back of his head. "You might say that," he said. "Depends on the time of day, I reckon."

John raised an eyebrow questioningly. "What do you mean by that?"

Specks shrugged his narrow shoulders slightly. "Jest that by day, it looks real peaceful."

John crossed his arms. "And at night?"

Specks nodded toward the grassland below. "And at night, it don't look so peaceful. That's when the ghost appears. 'Course, I ain't see'd it myself, mind you. But it sure put a burr under the saddle of some of the visiting dudes. They high-tailed it out o' here like they wuz being chased by a band o' rustlers."

Just then a peacock's cry pierced the quiet. *Ha-up! Ha-up!*

Specks waved his hands and yelled, "Whooop! Whoop! Git!" Turning back to John, he said, "When I get my ranch, I'll take rattlesnakes over those fancy-feathered turkeys any day of the week."

John grinned. "You plan on having your own ranch someday, do you?"

Specks nodded. "Sooner than someday. I'm planning on coming into plenty of money real fast. When I do, I'll get my own spread—breed horses, maybe."

Sebastian looked out at the grassland where the ghost supposedly had been seen. He felt his skin creep along his backbone. Those birds with their weird cry weren't making this any easier!

Specks left. John changed into his jeans and a Western shirt. He tugged on his boots. Laughing, he tied a red bandanna around Sebastian's neck.

"There now, old fellow," he said. "You look Western, too!"

A clanging sound came from the main house. Sebastian wagged his tail eagerly. Ah, at last. A real ranch meal! *Rrrrufpt!* he barked, urging John to hurry.

To Sebastian's dismay, he found that only John and Maude were eating in the dining room with the Culpeppers and the few remaining guests. He and Lady Sharon had their bowls—of dog food, yet!—in the dog run, a covered passage between the dining room and the kitchen.

Lady Sharon eagerly accepted her portion, nibbling daintily. But Sebastian was not to be denied his barbecue! How dare they feed the fuzzy gourmet this—this ordinary dog food! Hadn't he eaten in the best restaurants and the best fast-food drive-ins in the country?

Sebastian waited until the cook was putting out the garbage. Then he slipped into the kitchen and pulled a couple of T-bones off a platter on a side table. He gobbled the meat from them, then carried Lady Sharon the picked-clean bones for dessert. It took so little to satisfy that tasteless dog!

Lady Sharon wagged her stump of a tail and touched his nose with hers in gratitude. He wished she wouldn't do that! It was so embarrassing! Blushing through his fur, the irresistible canine carefully made his way toward the door to the dining room. Maybe he could eavesdrop and get some clues.

"Do you have any enemies, or have you gotten any threats lately?" John asked the Culpeppers.

Aunt Ethel ran her pudgy fingers through her blue hair. "No—that is, not really. Samuel Beher, owner of the spread next door, offered to buy us out. He wanted to add our place to the Lazy B Ranch and double his capacity. But he's been after us to sell out for the last fifteen years." She chuckled. "He thinks we're traitors for having a dude ranch instead of a real ranch."

John wrote in his notebook. "Maybe he got tired of waiting for you to sell to him," he said. "Why doesn't he like having, ah, dudes here?"

"None of it's true, of course, but he says they scare the horses and cattle, being kinda noisy," Uncle Bart said. "Oh, he's quick tempered and likes things to go his way," he added. "But he didn't mean anything by it, I'm sure. He always says that."

"Says what?" John asked.

"That if we don't sell out we'll regret it," Aunt Ethel said. She paused, frowning, then shrugged. "Bart's right. He always says that. He only means that we could lose our shirts depending on tourists, that's all. We don't pay any attention to him!"

"They've been friends for years," Maude said. "He talks like an old-time desperado, but he's really a dear man."

"His bark is worse than his bite," Bart said. "Just ask Specks!"

"Specks? The ranch hand?" John asked.

"Sure. He worked for Beher up until about six months ago. Worked for him for years."

"I'll talk to Specks tomorrow," John promised, pushing his chair back and standing. "For now, I'll leave you three to catch up on family talk. If I'm going to get an early start looking for your thieving ghost, I'd better get some sleep." He chuckled. "I guess here at the dude ranch I should say, catch some shut-eye."

Back at the cabin, Sebastian settled himself on the extra bed and listened to John snore softly. The peacocks had gone to sleep in the tree limbs. Their creepy cry was silenced for the night.

Sebastian drifted into a peaceful sleep, dreaming. He and John were being honored for catching the kidnapper and returning the horse. They were riding in a parade down Main Street. Confetti was raining on them, and—

Aaaaaaaaaaaaaah!

Suddenly, Sebastian sprang to his feet, alert and sniffing. He had heard a cry, not like the peacocks', but just as scary. He ran to the window and rose on his hind legs. He looked over the grassland, which was bathed in the soft moonlight.

His fur stood up on the nape of his neck and along the length of his spine. There, galloping at breakneck speed, was the ghost—or should he say *ghosts?*

4
Galloping Nightmare

Sebastian squeezed his eyes shut, then popped them open again. He hoped the apparition would be gone. But it was still there, glowing horribly as the shimmering horse and its silvery rider raced madly across the open ground.

An anguished whine escaped the lips of the old hairy hawkshaw.

"Wha-what is it, old fellow?" John muttered sleepily. "Come away from the window and be quiet. You'll wake the other guests."

Sebastian felt a bit braver now that John was awake. He emitted a low, rumbling growl, then glanced back to be sure John hadn't covered his head and gone back to sleep.

"What is it, boy?" John asked again. He slid from bed and howled angrily as he stubbed his toe on the unfamiliar bedpost. "This had better be good!" he said.

Sebastian felt John's hand on his neck as his human leaned over to look out the window with him.

"G-good grief!" John gasped. "It's—it's—"

John dashed to the cabin door and raced out into the night. "Ooooh!" he yelled, hopping back inside. "Don't ever go out in your bare feet up here!" he muttered. "Those stones are sharp as all get-out."

He grabbed his boots and yanked them on before running out again. But while John was struggling to get his boots on, Sebastian saw the apparition disappear behind some mesquite.

"Well, I guess the show's over, old fellow," John said, patting Sebastian and rubbing him under the chin.

Ummmmmm, Sebastian replied.

"There's no sense in going out there and stumbling in the dark. We'll look around in the morning."

It made good sense to Sebastian! He was not anxious to go sniffing about where that—that thing had been. The way it had glowed! He'd never seen anything like it in all his years of sleuthing. And he knew he didn't want to see it again! He'd rather be in the city, where the only horse he had to worry about was Royal Pain-in-the-Neck.

Sebastian slept restlessly the remainder of the night, several times getting up to look out the window. But there were no more sightings that night.

Just as darkness comes early in the hills, dawn comes late. *Ha-up! Ha-up!* Those peacocks greeted the dawn with the enthusiasm of roosters. Their spooky cry floated on the brisk, moist morning air.

Specks tapped on the door. He was carrying orange juice and coffee for John. "Breakfast is in an hour," he said. "You can eat in the dining room or by the river. Miss Culpepper suggested you might want to eat by the river at the cookout."

"How do I get there?" John asked, yawning.

"Trail ride," Specks said. "If you can't sit a horse, there's a hay wagon for the tenderfeet." He grinned mischievously, and his hundreds of freckles melted into one.

John squared his shoulders. "A horse will be fine. I—I remember riding one at the park when I was a little boy."

Specks turned to leave, chuckling to himself.

"Er, Specks," John said, "I understand you used to work at the Lazy B Ranch. What sort of fellow is Mr. Beher?"

Specks frowned. "Greedy." He trotted off without even commenting on the apparition of last night. Sebastian thought that was strange, though he remembered Specks's saying he'd never seen the ghost. Actually, that was even stranger.

John showered quickly and changed into his Western gear. Sebastian trotted alongside as they made their way down winding stone steps to the corral.

Maude and Lady Sharon greeted them. Then John and Maude selected their horses. The twelve remaining guests also mounted horses.

"Still quite a few guests," John told Maude.

She nodded. "Their cabins are on the other side of the ridge. They can't possibly see whatever it is. One of them even thought it was some sort of publicity stunt when he heard about it. Someone started a rumor that it was the ghost of a cowboy who'd mysteriously disappeared from a cattle drive in the 1800s."

Sebastian looked around. No horse for him? Was he expected to take the hay wagon or—worse yet—walk? He would never understand the thoughtlessness of humans.

The trail boss, whose name was Tiny, led them along narrow stone-strewn paths and then along a rocky creek bed. Sebastian certainly did not enjoy sloshing through water before breakfast, dodging horses' hooves. But at least he could smell the food cooking—sausage, bacon and eggs, and biscuits.

"Are we free to wander around on our own?" John called to Tiny.

Tiny obviously had gotten his name, as Specks had, from some teasing ranch hands. He was short and rode with his stirrups higher than most of the cowboys Sebastian had seen. The observant canine noticed, too, that he held the reins tight and short on the horse, unlike the more relaxed and confident hands on the ranch. He looked quite clumsy and amateurish, not at all like a true Westerner. Sebastian figured Tiny hadn't been riding as long as the rest of the ranch hands.

The trail boss yawned broadly. "You'd better

stick to the path," he said. "There might be snakes and wild animals. Even a cougar has been spotted now and then, I'm told."

"You're told?" John asked, voicing the same question that was forming in Sebastian's mind. "You've never seen one yourself?"

"I haven't been working here long," Tiny replied.

"Have you been a cowboy a long time, though?" John wondered aloud.

"I've been around horses all my life," Tiny said.

As they continued along the creek bed, Sebastian's keen eyes noticed the unmistakable U shape of horse tracks leading into the dense underbrush. He sniffed. But it was difficult for him to smell anything except breakfast at the moment.

Broken twigs—several of them only recently broken, as Sebastian could see from the oozing sap —testified that someone had indeed left the trail at that point. But who? And why? Hadn't Tiny said it might be dangerous to leave the trails? Of course, Tiny hadn't been working there long, he'd said. He probably didn't know what he was talking about. Sebastian made a mental note to follow the broken twigs later.

Ha-up! Ha-up! A peacock strutted from the underbrush. Could that big bird have broken the twigs?

Aaaaaaaaaah!

It was the same strange sound Sebastian had heard the night before—when the ghostly horse and rider had been on the grassland. It didn't seem close—it just floated on the morning air. But Sebastian's fur stood on end. Was that thing somewhere in the underbrush, hiding? Watching them, maybe?

He glanced ahead toward the trail riders. Apparently, they hadn't heard the sound, probably because of the clattering of the horses' hooves on the rocky creek bed.

Sebastian hurried to catch up with John. Lady Sharon seemed to think he was trying to reach her. She broke into a shy, panting grin.

He glared at her icily, then cocked a fuzzy ear toward John. John eased his horse up to Maude's and whispered, "Did you see it last night?"

She glanced around at the other riders before nodding. "I can see why people are leaving here in droves. It actually glowed. And it moved so fast."

"I know there's a logical explanation," John said. "But what?"

They came to the clearing at last, finally reaching the source of the delicious smell.

Sebastian was disgusted with the way Lady Sharon begged food from the guests. She sat up, offered her paw, rolled over, and flirted terribly for bits of sausage and gravied biscuits. Had she no pride?

He, on the other hand, was able to satisfy his own hunger by snatching plates of food the guests thoughtlessly left behind when they went to get more coffee.

After breakfast, the group rode back to the corral. John reserved a horse with which to explore the grassland where the ghost had been seen. "But do you have something more, er, ah, more comfortable?" he asked the wrangler. "This is quite different from a park pony."

While the wrangler was saddling up a horse more suited to John's riding ability—or inability—Sebastian decided to look on his own. He trotted out to the field where they had spotted the ghost the night before.

U-shaped tracks were everywhere. Whatever they had seen, it was not a ghost! Ghosts (that is, if there were such things as ghosts) leave no tracks.

But why would someone pretend to be a ghost? Was Beher, the owner of the Lazy B Ranch, trying to drive the Culpeppers out of business? Did he think he could frighten off all the guests and force the Culpeppers to sell out? But why take supplies? There wasn't enough taken at any one time to hurt business.

Sebastian looked up. To his dismay, there was Lady Sharon, trotting his way. How was a super detective like himself going to investigate properly with *her* tagging along all the time?

Sebastian pretended he didn't hear her yipping for him to wait and took off at a fast gallop. Any day he could outrace Lady Sharon! But he was going to have to find a disguise—that was all there was to it. He needed to hide from her and to snoop around unnoticed by the humans. And what went unnoticed around there more than anything else? A cowboy!

When Sebastian was sure he had lost Lady Sharon, he headed for the bunkhouse. He sneaked inside while the ranch hands were out tending the horses and doing other chores.

There, hanging on the wall, was a Western hat. He found a pair of boots beside one of the bunks. They had maps of Texas appliquéd on them and spurs already attached. Sebastian slipped them on. He saw his reflection in the mirror. What an authentic canine cowboy! How, he wondered, did he keep topping himself? Why, he looked just like John Wayne!

Bring on that phony ghost rider, that dirty sidewinder! Sebastian (Super Sleuth) was ready now.

5
Face to Face

Sebastian dogtrotted from the bunkhouse. He was heading for the hoofprints when somebody yelled.

"Hey, Tex!" Specks called. "Help me get this hay to the feed trough."

Sebastian glanced down at his boots with the map of Texas appliqués. Specks must mean him! There was little Sebastian could do except help. He didn't want to blow his disguise. He trotted out to the barn and pushed the bale of hay while Specks pulled and tugged.

"I guess you noticed—another bale of hay was missing this morning," Specks mumbled.

Sebastian nodded. *Errrrrrr*. Ummm, he thought. An interesting tidbit. Having this famous detective on the ranch hadn't deterred the criminal at all.

"I swear, you could feed a horse with what's

disappearing from around here," Specks grumbled. "And horse vitamins and liniment. Maybe one of the hands is going into business for himself, huh, Tex?"

Sebastian broke into a panting grin. *Huh, huh, huh.* The clever canine eyed Specks curiously. He had spoken of going into business for himself, and of getting the money for it soon. Maybe *he* was the ranch hand who was starting his own business with the Culpeppers' belongings. Sure, he'd called his former employer greedy, but that was probably just to throw the old hairy hawkshaw off the trail. Maybe Specks was still working for Mr. Beher —only now his job was sabotage.

At last, they got the bale to the trough. Specks spread it out, and the horses pushed and shoved one another to get to it.

Quickly, Sebastian slipped away before Specks could think of anything else for him to do. He hurried to the trail they had been on earlier. He followed the broken twigs until he saw hoofprints that went through the underbrush. His keen eyes spotted something strange about the prints. One horseshoe was nicked. All he had to do was find out whether Specks's horse was wearing a damaged shoe, and he'd know for sure if Specks was part of the so-called ghost.

The sun broke through the tree branches and bathed a group of fallen logs in bright light. Sebastian rose onto the logs and ran his nose along them, sniffing. Human and horse smells.

Suddenly, he picked up the sound of a horse's hooves coming that way. He sprang behind some low-growing mesquite and crouched down.

First, the horse's nose came into view, then the rider. It was Specks! He got down off his horse and knelt to brush his hand across the ground. Was he trying to wipe up prints? Specks scratched his chin, studying the ground. He squinted in Sebastian's direction.

The old super sleuth had to think quickly. *Arrr-ruu!* he howled, then skittered through the underbrush as quickly as he could, heading for the safety of the ranch house. He hoped his howl was close enough to the peacocks' cry to fool Specks.

Sebastian didn't stop until he was back at the main house. He saw John coming with Maude and ducked into the men's restroom next to the dining hall. He didn't want John to catch him in his disguise!

As the door shut behind him, Sebastian relaxed, but only for a moment. His fur stood on end. Standing directly across from him was the ghost!

Sebastian threw up his paws in terror, forgetting for a brief moment that he was a flawless, fearless canine. The ghost threw up his paws, too. Wait a minute! His paws?

Sebastian blinked and moved closer. He was looking at himself in a full-length mirror! But—but he *looked* like the ghost. He actually glowed, just as the ghost did. What had happened to make his paws and face glow?

Sebastian scanned his canine computer brain, searching for an answer. Suddenly, he knew. That strange growth on the logs was foxfire! Foxfire is a fungus that, unlike green plants, has no chlorophyll. It is a mold that lives on rotting wood and gives off a phosphorescent glow. Of course, he couldn't have noticed it when the sun was hitting it, he consoled himself. Sherlock Holmes himself would have missed it in the sunlight!

He was convinced that the ghost of the Bucking Bronc Dude Ranch was using that hidden pathway. But why? Where did it lead?

Sebastian had seen Specks on the trail before. He probably had gotten the foxfire glow there. Sebastian had to look at Specks's horse, to see if it wore a nicked horseshoe, and he had to find out where the trail led.

Sebastian washed his face and paws to get the foxfire off. He was about to leave when John

36

pushed into the men's room. "Oh, howdy," he told his furry partner. "Are you one of the hands? I believe Mrs. Culpepper is looking for someone to carry a gentleman's luggage."

Sebastian nodded, keeping his head low under the hat. He slipped into the lobby and stepped around some luggage. *Whew.* John hadn't recognized him.

A man in designer jeans and brand-new boots was at the registration desk. "And we won't stay here another night—not with that creepy thing out there," he was telling Ethel Culpepper.

"But I'm sure it's just someone's idea of a practical joke," Aunt Ethel told him.

"Well, it isn't very funny," the man said. "I came here for a rest. And I can't rest with that—that glowing thing racing around every night."

"Tex!" Aunt Ethel called to Sebastian. "Take Mr. Kelly's luggage to his car, please."

Obediently, Sebastian snatched the smaller piece of luggage between his teeth and trotted to the car that was parked in front by the house.

Lady Sharon ambled by, paying no attention to the handsome ranch hand. Sebastian smirked. She had no idea she had just passed the clever chameleon canine, the dog of her dreams!

The man picked up the larger piece of luggage,

tucked a newspaper under his arm, and followed
Sebastian, grumbling about the lost vacation.

"I might have been able to tell myself it was
only an animal making that terrible noise," the
man said. "But when I saw that—that awful ghost
horse and rider, I just couldn't stand it another
night."

He took the smaller piece of luggage from Sebastian and shoved it into his car trunk. Sebastian's keen eyes fell on the newspaper the man
carried under his arm. It was the *Dudetown Gazette*,
the local weekly newspaper. For some reason, it
looked familiar, although to Sebastian's knowledge
he'd never seen it before.

The clever canine stood watching as the man drove off without so much as a wave, a thank you —or a tip!

Sebastian growled under his breath. Humans! Still, the man had been a bit helpful. What had he said about the sound? An animal? Maybe. It wasn't a peacock's cry, and Sebastian didn't think it could come from a horse. Did Specks have some horrible animal out there in the woods that he brought out at night to scare people?

Sebastian wagged the stump of his tail. He was eager to follow that trail as far as it went and to get a good look at Specks's horse. Then maybe a lot of things would fall into place.

6
If the Shoe Fits

Clanga-clang! Sebastian licked his chops. He would solve this mystery, he was confident. But first things first. That was the dinner bell!

Sebastian took the opportunity afforded by his cowboy disguise to eat in the dining room. Let Lady Sharon deal with dog food; he'd take mesquite-broiled steaks and baked potatoes with yummy cheese and sour cream! Now, that was more suited to the furry gourmet's taste!

When he'd gobbled all he could (which was all there was!), he licked the remaining sauce and skedaddled to the barn.

He came to a screeching halt inside. Tiny was just nailing a shoe onto a cinnamon roan horse. It was Specks's horse! Sebastian glanced at a pile of discarded shoes. There was the nicked shoe. But then his keen eyes caught the gleam of new metal

40

on the hooves of no less than three horses, including Tiny's pinto and a chestnut horse with a blaze that Sebastian had seen one of the guests riding. He felt a terrible disappointment.

There was no way to make sure Specks's horse had been wearing the nicked shoe. He'd have to find another way to confirm that he was using the secret path.

"Doggone it!" Tiny complained. "And I paid good money for that hatband, too. Would you look at that, Tex?"

Sebastian scanned the hat that Tiny held in his hand. The hatband was made of silver conchas about the size of quarters, strung on a narrow band of leather. They were engraved with pictures of cowboy hats. From the looks of it, one of the conchas was missing.

"I special-ordered this. A day's wages, and the blame thing broke," Tiny moaned. "Guess it was while I was wrestling with one of these old buzzard-bait horses."

Sebastian shrugged sympathetically. *Ummmm.*

"Take that chestnut for a romp around the grounds," Tiny said. "He seems kinda restless."

Sebastian eyed the chestnut horse suspiciously. That was all he needed, a restless horse! Still, it would help maintain his cover as a cowboy. And it

41

would give him an excuse to ride out and take a look at that trail.

There was no way he could mount a horse as the humans did. He'd just have to improvise. Sebastian leaped over the rump of the horse and settled himself in the saddle.

Tiny laughed. "You been watching too many Roy Rogers movies. But that's not bad. Maybe the Culpeppers will let you do tricks for the guests. It might put extra pay in your check."

Sebastian snatched the reins between his teeth, and the chestnut took off. He was confident that he was a better rider than Tiny—any day! Fortunately, these horses knew the guest trails so well that he didn't have to do much guiding.

He bumped along, wondering what people saw in horseback riding, until he came to the cutoff. He leaped off and allowed the horse to continue on its customary trek.

Sebastian trotted cautiously along the trail, noting that some of the nicked hoofprints had been obscured by another set of hoofprints, as well as his own paw prints.

He kept his nose to the ground and followed the trail as it wound its way around trees, through shrubs, and into a clearing. This time he avoided rubbing against the foxfire.

Sebastian paused just in time. He nearly ran into a barbed-wire fence. On it there was a sign. It said: POSTED. KEEP OUT. PRIVATE PROPERTY. It had a *B* that looked as if it had been knocked over. That must stand for the Lazy B Ranch. The secret trail led right to the Lazy B Ranch and continued on the other side of the fence, maybe even to the ranch house itself!

He, Sebastian (Super Sleuth), had been right all along! Specks was working for Mr. Beher! Sebastian had to show John. But how was he going to get John to stop his own investigation and pay attention to him?

Sebastian had an idea. He would need Lady Sharon's help.

Of course, he couldn't let Lady Sharon know what was going on. Not that she would understand if she did know. But if he could get Lady Sharon to come along, he knew that Maude wouldn't be far behind. And with Maude there, John would be, too.

He smirked at his own cleverness as he raced back to the ranch. It was time to discard his disguise. This last bit of sleuthing called for his looking like his stupendous self.

When he got back to the bunkhouse, Tiny was outside, taking the saddle off the chestnut horse.

He laughed. "Threw you, did he? Happens to the best of us!" He laughed again.

Blushing because the man actually thought he, equestrian extraordinary, had been thrown from the horse, Sebastian slipped into the bunkhouse and discarded the clothes. It was especially insulting coming from such a clumsy cowboy as Tiny!

While Tiny was turning the horse into the corral, Sebastian skittered from the bunkhouse and back toward the grassy range, where he was sure John would be looking for clues.

He spotted John, Maude, and Lady Sharon. *Rrrrrrufpt!* he called to Lady Sharon.

She cocked her head, as if wondering whether he could really be calling her. Then she bounded toward him, leaping and spinning, yipping happily.

Sebastian turned and galloped toward the trail. Lady Sharon followed at full speed.

"Lady Sharon!" Maude called. "Come back!"

Maude spurred her horse to a full gallop, and John rode close behind, holding on as best he could and shouting, "Stop! I mean, whoa!"

Sebastian swerved into the cutoff and brushed past the foxfire-covered logs and through the underbrush, panting heavily as he led the trio closer and closer to the end of the trail.

45

He came to the barbed wire and skidded to a stop. Lady Sharon skidded, too, but not in time. She caught her fur on the barbs and let out a mighty howl.

Sebastian broke into a panting grin. He knew he could count on her klutziness to get Maude and John there!

Maude dismounted and ran to Lady Sharon. John came up, looking shaken and miserable, and finally managed to untangle himself from the horse's reins and stirrups.

While the two of them worked Lady Sharon

loose, Sebastian shimmied under the wire and onto the Lazy B.

"Sebastian! No, boy! Come back!" John shouted.

Sebastian barked and urged them to come on. Lady Sharon, now loose, shimmied under and joined in the chase, too.

"We've got to get her!" Maude shouted. "Look! The wires have been cut and rejoined here at this post. Let's go after them!"

Sebastian waited until he was sure John was on the Lazy B. Then he bounded along the trail, certain it would lead them right to Mr. Beher.

As he rounded the underbrush, though, he came to a skidding stop. He was face to face with Royal Pain-in-the-Neck and his goat companion!

7
The End of the Trail

The Thoroughbred reared and whinnied at the sudden intrusion. *Aaaaaaaaaa!* the goat cried, making the eerie sound that had frightened so many guests, including (blush, blush) the hairy hawkshaw himself.

Sebastian stared in disbelief. Could it be true? Could it be that the very racehorse they had been looking for in the city had been there—just acres away from them—that whole weekend? He knew now why the local paper had looked so familiar. He'd seen the same print in the ransom note!

The little goat, Snuffy, trotted up to the make-shift corral enclosing the horse. Sebastian sniffed. The corral was made of fallen logs and branches (covered with foxfire) tied together with rope, no doubt stolen from the Bucking Bronc Dude Ranch. Hay, probably also stolen from the ranch, was strewn about. Did that mean that the happen-

48

ings at the Bucking Bronc were only "fallout" from the horsenapping?

Lady Sharon, Maude, and John dashed up. "Oh, good grief!" John shouted. "It's—it's Royal Pain-in-the-Neck! Maude, do you realize what I've found?"

Sebastian glared icily at John. *I've* found? *Rrrrrrrr!*

"I've got to notify Chief at once!" John said. "Oh, Maude, this means that I'll be off Chief's mad list!"

We, John, Sebastian thought. We! It was so hard to get humans to share the credit.

"When I saw that newspaper in the lobby with the old-fashioned print, I should have realized it was the same as the ransom note!" John groaned.

Shouldn't they both? the chagrined canine thought. He guessed he couldn't blame John too much for that little oversight. Even he, incredible sleuth that he was, had missed it at first.

Maude approached the horse carefully, talking gently to it. She looked at Royal's eyes, pulled back his lips, and looked in his mouth. Then she patted his flanks. "He's been well taken care of," she said. "He looks as if he's been exercised every day."

Every *night,* Sebastian thought. He was the bottom half of the galloping ghost of the Bucking Bronc Dude Ranch.

"Beher must've kidnapped the horse," John said. "Specks said he was greedy."

Maybe Beher wasn't in on it at all, Sebastian thought. If the glow of the horse and rider had been accidentally caused by brushing against the foxfire, it probably was not intended to scare off the Culpeppers. No, Beher most likely was not in on this. It was Specks's doing.

Specks had worked for Beher for a long time. That was how he knew that that was a deserted part of the ranch and that no one would find the horse there. And, as for the money he said he'd be coming into, he must have meant the ransom money for Royal Pain-in-the-Neck.

"The job is only half done," John said. "I've got to locate the horsenapper."

The sun disappeared behind the hills, casting deep shadows over the area. In the duller light, Sebastian and Lady Sharon, the fence, and the horse cast an eerie glow.

"Look, John!" Maude gasped. "The dogs!"

John snapped his fingers. "Foxfire! Being a city boy, I had completely forgotten. But once, when I was a Boy Scout and went camping, some of us found a log covered with foxfire. We rubbed ourselves with it and tried to scare the other kids. That explains the glowing figure on the glowing horse."

Sebastian scratched his ear. He would have to forgive John for being slow. Even the very best detectives miss little clues at first. Hadn't the cunning canine, the curse of criminals everywhere, not noticed it until he'd come face to face with it in the mirror?

"Whoever took Royal was exercising him every night," John continued. "He might have gone completely undetected, except for the foxfire glowing and scaring the guests. At least Royal will be in good shape for the race," he said.

Sebastian wagged the stub of his tail. He touched his cold nose to John's hand, encouraging him to continue. John was on a roll!

"It's somebody who knows racehorses," John said.

Sebastian broke into a panting grin. Specks knew horses. Maybe not racehorses, but horses. Close enough.

"Someone who knows how to take care of Royal, who knows enough to keep his goat with him," John continued.

Sebastian nibbled at a burr caught in his fur. Specks probably knew that.

Just then, Sebastian picked up the sound of thrashing feet. With spurs. John heard it, too. He motioned for Maude to be quiet.

Suddenly, Specks burst through the underbrush.

"Wha— I don't know what you folks are doing over here in Mr. Beher's territory, but he don't cotton to trespassers."

"And what are you doing here?" John asked. "Did you come to feed Royal Pain-in-the-Neck?"

"Royal what?" Specks asked, tilting his hat forward to scratch his head.

"Then you don't know—"

"All I know is, I was sure I saw Tex slipping off into the woods earlier, goofing off from work. Then he disappeared again, and I decided to look for him. Next thing, I spotted y'all and followed. Dudes can get in a powerful lot of trouble out here alone. And I don't think Mr. Beher would appreciate y'all bothering his horse. If he wants it way out here, then that's his concern."

John waved his hands. "This is *not* Mr. Beher's horse. This is the horsenapped Thoroughbred!"

"What horsenapped Thoroughbred?" Specks asked. "You city folks talk in riddles."

If Specks wasn't the horsenapper, what about the money he bragged he was coming into soon? Sebastian wondered.

"What about the money you mentioned?" John voiced Sebastian's thoughts.

Specks grinned. "Mr. Beher's gonna finally pay me all the back wages he owes me. If he hadn't fell so fer behind in the first place, I'd still 'a' been workin' fer him."

Sebastian rolled to a half-sitting position to scratch his ear. If Specks wasn't the horsenapper, then who— He spotted something in the dust.

It was a concha! And it had little Western hats engraved on it. Tiny! Of course! He did say he'd been around horses all his life. Maybe he didn't mean saddle horses! Tiny knew horses, and he was small enough to be a jockey. Suddenly, an image flashed through the clever canine's mind—Tiny used his stirrups high. And he held the reins differently, too. While it was clumsy for a cowboy, it was perfect for a jockey.

He had to help John find this clue. Sebastian pawed at the concha. He barked at it and pushed it with his nose.

"What is it, boy?" John asked. "We can't play games now."

Play? Was that all John thought him capable of? Shame, John!

Sebastian barked at the concha again. He spread-eagled in front of it and barked until John came over.

"Here, now," John said, stooping to pick up the concha. "What's this?"

John held up the concha.

Specks moved forward to examine it. "I know that from somewhere," he said, scratching his chin thoughtfully.

Go on, Sebastian thought impatiently. Think, Specks!

Sebastian picked up another scent. Then he caught the faint rustling in the bushes. Someone else was coming. But then the sound lessened, which told him the person had changed his mind; he was turning away. It had to be Tiny. No doubt he had seen them and knew that the horse had been found. He would disappear from sight, and John would never know. He, Sebastian (Super Sleuth), had to do something—and fast.

Sebastian sprang into the bushes, knocking Tiny to the ground. He grabbed the hat. Tiny grabbed back. Sebastian tugged harder. *Errrrrrr.*

"Leggo, you stupid mutt," Tiny yelled. "Leggo my hat."

John stepped from around the bush and grabbed Tiny. "Ah, ha!" he yelled.

"I—I was following Specks," Tiny said. "I thought maybe I could find out if he was the ghost rider of the Bucking Bronc."

"This is getting ridiculous," John said, handing Tiny's hat back to him. "Lady Sharon followed Sebastian, Maude followed Lady Sharon, I followed Maude, Specks followed me, and you followed Specks. It seems that everyone has come but the kidnapper!"

The hat! Sebastian thought. Why didn't John look at the hat! The hairy hawkshaw snapped at the hat again, tugging it from Tiny.

"Stop that, Sebastian! Bad do— Here, what's this?" John asked. He pulled the concha from his pocket and held it next to the hatband. It fit perfectly in the empty space.

"This concha was in the corral with the kidnapped horse," John said. "It was there when we arrived. This means that you've been here before. While I have no official jurisdiction here," John continued, "I am performing a citizen's arrest until the sheriff can be notified. And I'm sure he'll be glad to extradite you to the city on the charges of horsenapping and extortion."

Sebastian licked John's hand. He was so glad that John had really done it—with a lot of help from his furry partner, naturally.

On questioning him, they learned that Tiny's real name was Cary Staar. He had once been Royal Pain-in-the-Neck's jockey, but he'd been fired by the owners. He hadn't been able to get another job racing and had decided to kidnap the horse.

Tiny was originally from around there (that explained why he spoke "cowboy" so well, Sebastian concluded) and knew the lay of the land—including Beher's. He knew it was a good area to hide a horse in and especially liked that it was close to the city. After all, one couldn't travel too far with an easily recognizable horse in a rented or stolen horse trailer! So he got himself a job at the dude ranch and proceeded to carry out his plan.

Even if the owners hadn't paid the ransom

money, Staar said, he would have returned the horse just before the race. He'd planned to tell them that he'd been following leads on his own and found the horse in a barn outside the city. He'd figured they'd be so grateful, maybe they'd give him his old job back.

"It was just an accident that people thought there was a ghost," Tiny said. "But I wasn't sorry. It meant there'd be fewer people here to discover my secret."

When one of those people was a cagey canine, no more were needed, Sebastian thought smugly as he scratched a burr from his fur.

Hmmmmmm, the hairy hawkshaw muttered to himself. He'd certainly been fooled into thinking that Specks was the guilty one. Especially because Specks had never seen the ghost! That had seemed awfully suspicious. Under John's questioning, however, Specks said the reason was that he was so tired at night he could sleep through a thunderstorm.

The only drawback in solving this case so quickly and handily, as Sebastian could see it, was now they'd have to hurry back to the city with Royal and Tiny. That meant missing a delicious ranch supper. But the Culpeppers were so grateful for the solution to their ghost mystery that they gave John barbecue and beans to take home.

"Take this doggie bag, with our appreciation," they said.

Sebastian wouldn't soon forget the look on Chief's face when they pulled up in front of the police station with the horsenapped Thoroughbred in a borrowed trailer and the horsenapper in handcuffs.

Police were everywhere in the city, scouring yards and parks, but the hairy hawkshaw and his human had solved the whole thing! News photographers took pictures of them returning the horse to the owners. Of course, Chief jumped into the pictures, too. And when the reporters asked why all the other police had stayed in town while John had gone to the dude ranch, Chief told the reporters that he'd sent John undercover to check out the countryside.

"I guess that means I get paid overtime for these days, huh, Chief?" John said.

Chief grumbled, but he had to agree, because all the reporters were still listening.

After the excitement had died down, Maude took John and Sebastian home. Lady Sharon touched Sebastian's nose in farewell. It was so embarrassing! *Errrrrrrr.*

"Why don't you and Lady Sharon come in for

supper?" John asked. "I'll just heat up the beans and barbecue your aunt and unc— What?"

John pulled the seat down and looked all around the back of the station wagon. "Where on earth did it all go?" he asked. "Did I forget to load it in the wagon?"

Sebastian broke into a panting grin, trying to look as innocent as he could (one of his better disguises). His fuzzy face spread in a panting grin. Hadn't the Culpeppers called it a *doggie* bag?

Buu-uuurp!